The Adventures of Octavia and Fortepiano

Part One:
Troublesome Triplets

Ann Warner

HALLMARK PRESS

Published by Hallmark Press

The sign of a quality publication

www.hallmarkpress.co.uk

Published in the United Kingdom by Hallmark Press, 2007

Edited by Sheila Seacroft

Cover design by Lintons, Prospect Road, Crook, Co. Durham

Typeset by TW Typesetting, Plymouth, Devon

Printed by Antony Rowe, Eastbourne, Sussex

Dedication

To David, wherever you are.

In memory also of my Dad who taught me to love books.

Acknowledgements

To Ken, my husband, whose love and encouragement has kept me writing; and to all the children of Halkirk past and present who have inspired me.

Little does Octavia know, but her surprise birthday gift from her Grandmother is a grand piano; but this piano is much more than it seems.

Fortepiano, for that is what her piano is called, is very much a person in his own right. Little does our friendly piano realise, but he has lodgers under his strings. They are called the Triplets; Poco, Pochettino (Poch for short), and Placido, all three very mischievous little people.

This story is all about how the Triplets cause a lot of trouble for not only Fortepiano and Octavia, but also Octavia's music teacher, Mrs Lines.

Chapter 1

Today was the day! Octavia Brown was sitting on her front doorstep waiting. Her two big white Samoyed dogs, Storm and Jazz, were beside her. They sensed something big was about to happen from the way Octavia kept jumping up and then sitting down again, and generally not settling. For this was Octavia's big day. Her tenth birthday had arrived and her Grandmother had promised her a very special birthday present. Octavia had thought long and hard for days about what this surprise present might be. Maybe a trip to Disneyworld; now wouldn't that be something! But Grandma wasn't able to travel very far, so she wouldn't be able to go, and it wouldn't be fun without her. For Grandma was always so full of fun. Every time she came to visit, or Octavia went to visit Grandma, it was always lots of fun and laughter with plenty of interesting things to do. So a trip to Disneyworld might not be the best present.

So what could Grandma be sending her? Grandma lived in the big city of Edinburgh. It was a long way from where Octavia lived, for she lived in a village in Caithness, which was in the far North of Scotland. It took five long hours in a car for Octavia to go and visit Grandma. When she had spoken to her on the telephone Grandma had told her her surprise present wasn't coming by post. It was coming all the way from Edinburgh in a van which Octavia was to look out for on the day of her birthday. Octavia was to look out for a big yellow van with a picture painted on its side; when Octavia saw what it was she might be able to guess what her surprise present might be. So Octavia just couldn't wait for this van to arrive at her door. She had been waiting and listening for it all morning; now it was lunchtime and it still hadn't arrived! How long could five hours be, she thought to herself!

'Come on, it's lunchtime,' shouted her mother from the kitchen. 'You have to eat, Octavia.' But Octavia couldn't move from the front door. She had now sat down on a chair by the glass door, where she could see better. She was just about big enough to see down the long driveway to the road if she sat up very straight on the chair. It had to come soon, it just had to, or she would burst with excitement!

'Come and have your lunch, Octavia,' called her mother again. 'Sitting out there won't make it come any quicker.'

Oh well, thought Octavia, if I have my lunch, it will pass the time. So off she went to the kitchen with her two dogs by her side. As she ate, she just couldn't stop thinking about where the yellow van would be now. She hurried her lunch so fast, her mother told her she would make herself sick. I don't care, she thought, at least if I eat quickly I'll get back to my seat at the door. Then Octavia had a brilliant thought. Surely Grandma would have told her mother what her birthday surprise was! That was it, she would see if she could trick her mother into telling her, or even give her a hint at what it might be. 'Mum,' she said, in a voice she thought Mum might listen to. 'Mum, Grandma must have told you what my surprise is. Couldn't you just give me a tiny, tiny, little clue?'

'What would be the good of that,' answered her mother, 'it wouldn't be a surprise then, would it, and you might guess what it was!'

'But how can I possibly guess,' whined Octavia in her best whiny voice. 'I don't have any idea what Grandma is sending me.'

'Oh don't you . . .' said her mother in a very mysterious voice.

Now, thought Octavia, what have I forgotten about that I might like to have? And she began to puzzle over this momentous problem. While she was thinking about this the big yellow van arrived at the door!

The first Octavia and her mother knew something was happening was when her two dogs started barking. Octavia rushed across the hall to the door, nearly falling over Storm and Jazz on the way! Then Octavia had the door opened before her mother could get there. Out she went to where the van was parked, trying to see what was painted on its side as she went. Wow, she said to herself, for there, painted on the side of the van, was a picture of a grand piano! Above the picture was written in big black letters: Ebony and Ivory, Tuning, Repairs, Sales. Professional Tuners throughout Scotland. Proprietor, Mr C. Sharp. M.I.M.I.T. Now she understood! Clever, wonderful, oh so kind Grandma had sent her a piano for her birthday! She remembered now, she had told Grandma ages ago she longed to learn to play the piano. But she couldn't, because she didn't have a piano to practise on. Now, her dream had come true thanks to Grandma. Octavia could hardly wait for Mr Sharp to take the piano out of the van. 'Is there a little girl living here with a birthday today?' he teased.

'Yes, yes!' shouted Octavia jumping up in the air. 'That's me!'

Then Mr Sharp opened the doors of his van. All Octavia could see was – wait a minute – all Octavia could see *were* three very large wooden legs, and a big flat object covered with a cloth. That can't be my piano, she thought to herself, peering into the dark of the van. Seeing the puzzled look on Octavia's face, Mr Sharp explained that as Grandma had sent her a small grandpiano, it had to be carried in two parts. Octavia was both very relieved and very excited at the same time. To be given a piano as a present was wonderful, but to be given a *grand* piano, well that was a definite WOW! She would have to work extra hard at practising to make Grandma proud of her. So Octavia watched as Mr Sharp took her piano very carefully out of his van and into the house. Octavia's dad had to help as Mr Sharp had brought it on his own. 'Careful. Watch the step,' said Mr Sharp.

'I've got it,' replied Octavia's dad.

'I think we'll have it in here in the sitting room,' said Mrs Brown. 'Just there in the corner beside the window.'

Octavia and her mum watched as the piano was put on its three big legs, and set very carefully in the corner of the room. How lovely and shiny it looks, thought Octavia to herself, longing to touch the gleaming white keys. 'Go on,' said Mr Sharp, 'have a go.'

Octavia's face fell, 'I can't,' she replied, 'I don't know how to play yet, but I'm going to learn!' she said excitedly. So Mr Sharp offered to play a tune for her, while Octavia stood and watched and listened. It has such a beautiful sound, thought Octavia. And she hoped that someday she could play as well too.

Mr Sharp explained to Mr and Mrs Brown that he would come back in a month's time to tune the piano properly. 'Best let it get used to its new home first,' he said. Then Octavia and her parents went to the door to say good-bye to Mr Sharp. As soon as Mr Sharp's van had disappeared down the drive Octavia had rushed back inside to have another look at her beautiful piano. Mr and Mrs Brown came back into the room too to have another look. 'Oh I'm so lucky,' she said to them. 'This has been the best birthday ever!'

'I'm so glad you are pleased,' said her mother. 'But don't you think you should go and phone Grandma? She will want to know your piano has arrived safely. And remember to say thank you!'

Octavia felt terrible, she had been so busy thinking about her new piano, and that now she would be able to have piano lessons, she had completely forgotten about dear Grandma!

So off she went to phone her, and to thank her for her wonderful birthday surprise!

Chapter 2

Now Fortepiano, that was his name, was very pleased to have arrived. It wasn't very nice standing on your side for five hours having your keys jingled all over the place! Fortepiano was delighted with himself. What a lovely room to stay in, he thought. It had two big windows which let the sun in and made it a happy room to be in. And what a lovely little girl. We'll play well together – only – well – she doesn't know that I'm very special, he thought to himself. And so he was, a very special piano. Even in the workshop where he had been made Fortepiano had been special. He was often worked on longer than the other pianos, his wood was varnished and polished till it shone. His keys were checked over and over by Peter who made him. He looked very special, he sounded very special. So it was no wonder that when Grandma Williamson saw him in Mr Sharp's shop, she knew right away Fortepiano was the one for her dear grand-daughter Octavia!

What, you might ask, was so special about Fortepiano? Well, he thought he was a magic piano! He could do things other pianos couldn't do. He could make his keys go up and down to play a tune! He had found this out about himself when he was in the workshop. Suddenly his hammers began to move up to hit his strings – then – wow, he was playing a tune all by himself, no one was touching him to make him play. So he thought, I'm extra special, I'm magic. I can play tunes without anyone hitting my keys!

Now Fortepiano might have had quite different thoughts if he had known who really had been playing with his keys, and who, at this moment, was fast asleep beneath his strings!

Chapter 3

Phew! They were tired! They had travelled all the way from Edinburgh with Fortepiano; of course he didn't know yet he had guests! Poco, Poch, which was short for Pochettino, and Placido lay fast asleep under Fortepiano's strings! What a journey they'd had, for they had to hang upside down most of the way, and now the Triplets, that's what they called themselves, were exhausted! The Triplets were the 'little people' of the musical world. They were about the size of a musical note, and they wore black trousers and white jackets. On their heads they wore little flat black hats, just like pieces of board, so when they walked under a piano's strings they didn't catch on any. Triplets appeared whenever they heard music, especially music that wasn't being played very well. This meant that for some of the time they became very bored. Triplets should have been helpful, but a lot of the time they were inside a piano they got up to mischief and made keys that were being played sound out of tune. They were, you see, quite naughty and unruly. When they got up to mischief inside a piano and made things not sound right they had a wheezy, tinkly, laugh. Pianos didn't particularly like having them around, and of course Fortepiano, being a new piano, didn't yet know about these musical little pests called Triplets! So there they were fast asleep under his strings. How, you might ask, did they get there? Well they lived in the workshop where Fortepiano was made. Their house was an old wooden metronome which stood on a window ledge in the piano workshop. When all the men who made the pianos went home each night, the Triplets came out to play. One night they stayed out to play too late, and had to jump into Fortepiano before Peter the piano maker found them next morning.

They were stuck inside Fortepiano, and since it was much nicer and roomier living under his strings, for he had over two hundred strings, than living in a metronome, they decided to stay.

Now Poco, Poch, and Plæcido were fast asleep, and poor Fortepiano was, for the moment, unaware of the trouble brewing under his strings!

Chapter 4

Octavia sat at her piano dreaming. Maybe some day she would be so good at playing the piano, she would be asked to play in somewhere like the Albert Hall! She had seen concerts there on the television. And she could just picture it, playing with a big orchestra, then the audience clapping. Or she might be a piano teacher, or . . . 'Octavia,' said her mother, coming into the sitting-room. 'Stop sitting there dreaming, that won't get you a piano teacher. Come on, it's time to go.' Mrs Brown was taking Octavia to see Mrs Lines the piano teacher who lived in a cottage just outside the village. She lived there on her own with her cat for company. Every weekday after school was finished for the day she took boys and girls for piano lessons. Octavia had heard from her friends at school that Mrs Lines was quite a strict teacher, but she was, they thought, good at teaching. So although Octavia was looking forward to meeting her, she was also a bit scared, and she hoped she wouldn't be too frightening. Mrs Brown got her coat on, gave the dogs some doggy biscuits, and told them to be good till she and Octavia got back, made sure Octavia was neat and tidy, and off they went in Mrs Brown's little red car. Octavia was very excited, and in no time at all they had arrived at Mrs Lines' cottage. 'Here we are,' said her mother, and Octavia knew right away they were there because carved into the wooden gate at the top was a treble clef and lots of musical notes. Octavia recognised them from learning recorder at school.

Mrs Brown and Octavia went up the little path to the door. It didn't have a door bell; it had a lovely brass door knocker instead in the shape of a treble clef. Octavia was allowed to give the door one rap. In no time at all Mrs Lines answered it and was asking them into her sitting-room which led straight from the front door. Octavia shook hands with Mrs Lines – she had to bend her head quite a way back to look up at her – as Mrs Lines was quite tall.

When Octavia looked up at her she noticed she had very blue eyes, and wore glasses with large bright pink frames. Very fashionable, thought Octavia to herself. 'So,' said Mrs Lines, 'you would like me to teach you to play the piano?'

'Yes please,' replied Octavia, trying to be very polite, in case Mrs Lines didn't like her and refused. 'I would like very much to learn to play the piano, more than I would like to do anything else.'

'Have you a piano?' asked Mrs Lines. Before Octavia could answer, her mother explained that Octavia had just been given the present of a new grand piano for her birthday, from her Grandmother. 'A grand piano,' exclaimed Mrs Lines. 'You are a very lucky girl!'

'Oh yes,' said Octavia, 'I can't wait to learn to play it.' Then while her mother and Mrs Lines made arrangements for Octavia's lessons, Octavia looked about her at Mrs Lines sitting-room. Against one wall of course was the piano, an upright piano. It's not as nice or as beautiful as my piano, thought Octavia. I hope ... just then Octavia's mother interrupted her thoughts. 'How would you like Mrs Lines to give you lessons on your own piano, Octavia?' Octavia was speechless, for she secretly wasn't looking forward to having lessons here at Mrs Lines' cottage. She couldn't quite put her finger on it, but being in Mrs Lines' sitting-room gave her a funny feeling.

'Oh yes please!' she replied. 'I'd really like that.' So it was arranged that every Saturday morning at eleven o'clock Mrs Lines would be at Octavia's house to give her lessons.

Mrs Lines then explained to Octavia which book she would need to buy for beginning lessons. And after saying thank you again to Mrs Lines, Octavia and her mother set off for home. It's really happening, thought Octavia as they drove home. I'm really going to learn to play the piano! Then she thought again of dear Grandma in Edinburgh. Without her all of this wouldn't be happening. Wait till I tell her I'm having my first piano lesson on Saturday . . .

Chapter 5

The sun was shining, the birds were singing outside the window, and Fortepiano sitting in his corner had never been happier. All that would make his happiness complete would be if someone would come and play him. He hadn't felt magical for days now, so he began to wonder if he had really been able to make his keys play a tune or if he had been imagining it. So he tried jiggling them a bit, but nothing happened. So he tried again, still nothing happened. Oh dear, he thought, I'm right. I'm not a magic piano after all!

While Fortepiano had been trying to jiggle his keys up and down to play a tune, the Triplets had been wakened up with all the clicking and jiggling Fortepiano was doing. 'What's going on?' whispered Poco to the other two.

'I'm too tired to bother,' said Poch.

'And I'm not really interested,' said Placido.

Poco then gave the two of them a really good shake. 'But where are we?' he asked them. 'We've stopped moving, we must be somewhere.'

'Oh be quiet,' said Poch again. 'Just let me sleep.'

'Well I'm going to find out,' replied Poco, and he stood up too quickly and immediately hit his head on one of Fortepiano's strings! 'Ouch! That hurt,' he said, and immediately sat down again. Then he saw his hat had fallen off, no wonder it hurt! So he put his little flat hat back on again, and very carefully this time stood up. That was much better, now he could have a look around. Well, at least we are still inside the piano, he thought to himself. Poco took a walk to one end of Fortepiano and had a look over the edge, then he saw Octavia sitting on the piano stool gazing lovingly at Fortepiano. Mmm. Thought so, the piano belongs to a 'Tendernote'. That was the Triplets' name for a learner. Or, he thought to himself, she might be a 'Virtuoso'. That was their name for someone who could play the piano really well. I wonder which she is, he thought. Then when he'd seen enough, he ran back to where the other two were still lying snoozing. 'Wake up you two!' and he gave Poch and Placido another shake.

'Go away,' they both said at once. But Poco persisted in trying to get their attention, and so eventually Poch opened his eyes, yawning and stretching his little arms and legs. Placido, though, kept on dozing. 'What do you want?' asked Poch very sleepily. 'I'm fed up with you keeping trying to waken me.'

'Don't be so stupid and boring,' replied Poco. 'I've found out where we are.'

'Oh, all right then,' answered Poch, 'Where are we?'

'Well,' said Poco, 'I think we've landed on our feet this time.'

'What do you mean?' asked Poch.

'Well, we seem to be in the house of a "Tendernote", or maybe a "Virtuoso", I'm not sure yet. I've seen a little girl, so maybe she's a "Tendernote",' he said.

Poch thought about this piece of news for a moment, then his little eyes began to dance with mischief, and his little feet jumped up and down with excitement. 'Oh good, now we can have some fun again, it's a long time since we had some really good fun,' he said wistfully. For the Triplets had been hiding in Fortepiano for some time, not knowing what was going to happen, and they were becoming rather fed up and bored now with doing nothing but sitting under Fortepiano's strings. They had quite forgotten it was their fault they had got stuck there in the first place!

Now Fortepiano wouldn't have been very pleased if he'd known just then what was going on under his strings, because he was dreaming about being magical again. He was dreaming about being able to do wonderful things like making beautiful music with his keys.

He was also, if the truth were told, becoming very bored with his own company. All the excitement of arriving at his new home had worn off, all he wanted now was someone to come and play some nice tunes on his keys. For at the moment, all he did was sit all day in his corner, and he was beginning to feel a tiny bit abandoned, and was afraid that in fact he would just be left to sit there all day, every day, with no one bothering about him! But of course he hadn't been abandoned. In more ways than one very soon he was going to find he had lots of company, and some of that he was going to wish he didn't have!

Chapter 6

Saturday morning was here at last! Octavia had been counting the days till her first piano lesson. Now her big day had arrived and she couldn't wait for it to be eleven o'clock! 'Make sure you wash your hands,' said her mother. 'You don't want to get anything nasty on those nice new piano keys!' Octavia rushed off upstairs to wash her hands, in fact she washed them twice over, just in case she had missed anything nasty! Then she went into her bedroom and sat down in front of her dressing-table mirror to make sure there were no dirty smudges on her face, and to check her hair was neat and tidy. Yes, she looked fine. Then off she ran downstairs to the kitchen where her dad and mum were having a cup of coffee, to wait for Mrs Lines. 'Come and sit down and have a drink while you are waiting,' said Mr Brown. But Octavia wasn't really listening to him, she was listening for the door bell. 'Octavia,' said her mother, 'didn't you hear what your dad said?'

'Sorry,' replied Octavia. 'I wasn't listening!' Her dad and mum smiled at each other. Of course they knew that she wasn't listening! She was too excited to listen to either of them. Jazz and Storm seemed to know too that Octavia had something on her mind, for they kept nudging her with their big wet noses; but today Jazz and Storm weren't a priority with Octavia, learning to play the piano was. So they sat down, one on either side of her with their heads on her lap, while she sat absentmindedly patting them. At exactly eleven o'clock the door bell rang, but Octavia didn't move. She sat quite still on her seat, frozen it seemed with excitement. She couldn't get her legs to work! 'Come on Octavia,' said Mr Brown. 'Answer the door, that will be Mrs Lines.' Octavia suddenly seemed to come out of her dreamlike state, and then dashed out of the kitchen and ran to the door.

It's at last going to happen, she thought. Today is really here! Then she opened the door to Mrs Lines, saying 'Good-morning', in a very polite but rather high and excited voice.

'Hello Octavia,' replied Mrs Lines. 'Are you looking forward to your first piano lesson?'

'Oh yes, I can't wait,' said Octavia, and she very politely showed Mrs Lines into the sitting-room where Fortepiano sat in his corner looking beautiful and shiny in the morning sunlight, if not feeling rather gloomy! That was, until he saw Octavia and Mrs Lines. Ah, he thought, something is going to happen to me at last. And he prepared himself to be played!

Chapter 7

Mrs Lines settled Octavia on the piano stool and sat down on the stool which Mrs Brown had put there for her, beside the piano. Then Octavia's first ever piano lesson began! At first Octavia was so excited she couldn't take in all the information Mrs Lines was giving her. There were the names of the lines and spaces, and all about the treble clef and bass clef. Everything Octavia needed to know to start her off playing the piano. Oh dear, thought Octavia to herself, what a lot to learn and remember. While she was trying to take all this in, Mrs Lines told her to turn to the first page of her book, then she showed her the names of the first notes she was to learn and where to find them on Fortepiano's keys. Then Octavia was allowed to play a little tune with the notes she had just learned. Oh gosh, there was a lot to remember at first, Octavia was thinking. But if she practised and learned it all properly, Mrs Lines told her, she would pick it up in no time. Octavia was eager to learn, so when it came to the end of the lesson, she asked if she could go on to the next two pages in her piano book, if she could manage them, before the next lesson. 'Certainly,' said Mrs Lines, very pleased at how keen Octavia was. 'But remember,' she went on, 'what I taught you about the rhythm and counting as you play.' Octavia promised she would try to do everything Mrs Lines had just taught her that morning. And then her first lesson was over and Mrs Lines was off home. Once Octavia had shown Mrs Lines out she ran to the kitchen to tell her parents how her first lesson had gone. In fact she was so excited about it, she could hardly get the words out to tell them everything.

'I'm so pleased that you enjoyed it,' said Mrs Brown. 'Just make sure you keep practising,' said Mr Brown. And Octavia did just that, she ran from the kitchen back to her beloved piano, who was waiting for her. He was feeling more like a real piano now, he was going to be played and practised on often, he could just feel it. He was so happy he nearly played a quick scale on his own! At last he was being used for what he'd been made for, life couldn't be better. But maybe he was being a bit too cheerful about that!

While Octavia had been having her first piano lesson the Triplets had been sitting very quietly under Fortepiano's strings listening. In fact they had never sat so quietly for a long time, probably not since they had lived in the piano workshop and had to be very quiet during the day when people were in working on the pianos. But this morning was special, it was the little Tendernote's first piano lesson, and they didn't want to spoil that. 'She's definitely a "Tendernote",' said Poco.

'She's going to learn fast though,' replied Placido.

'I think I am going to like our little Tendernote,' said Poco.

'Mmm,' answered Poch. 'But I don't like her teacher, we'll have to watch her very carefully.'

'We can have such fun now,' said Poco. 'Think of all the things we can help little Tendernote with.'

'Or not!' replied Poch. After Octavia had left the sitting-room the Triplets had done a little dance up and down Fortepiano's hammers, for sitting quietly for too long was not in their nature. Dancing on the hammers had made them hit the strings so it sounded like a real tune was being played, and that was what had perked up Fortepiano to thinking he was magic again and could play tunes on his own! Of course he still hadn't realised he had lodgers! And Octavia had no idea either. Just as well she didn't suspect anything, for little did she know the crisis her next piano lesson would bring!

Chapter 8

Octavia loved her piano lessons. Each week she longed for Saturday to come round so it would be lesson time again. She was practising hard and in no time at all she had learned all the things Mrs Lines had taught her at the first lesson. She could name all the lines and spaces on the music, and of course she had learned the names of Fortepiano's keys very quickly. This, she knew was very important, and she loved pressing each key down to hear the different sounds that came from each note. Of course there were bits she found difficult, like remembering that the order of the lines and spaces was different in the bass clef from the treble clef. And the first little tune she played from her book where you had to play both hands together was just frightening and exciting all at the same time. Life, though, on the whole, was really good for Octavia now she had her piano, and when her class teacher at school heard she was learning to play the piano, she'd said that when Octavia had had more lessons, she'd like her to play something to the class. Octavia was delighted; this meant she would be practising extra hard to learn all she could, so she could play at school to her classmates and teacher. For, after all, wasn't one of her dreams to be so good she could play to other people? Of course she never forgot it was all thanks to her dear Grandma, she was the one who was helping to make her dreams come true! In fact when she had last spoken to Grandma on the phone, Grandma had told her she and Grandpa would be coming up soon to visit, and they were looking forward to hearing her play. Octavia was very excited when she heard this. Every day she practised hard, and every Saturday when Mrs Lines came for the lesson, she said what a difference she heard in Octavia's playing!

That was until one Saturday when during the lesson Octavia's playing seemed to go quite horribly wrong! Every time she began playing one of her tunes, the notes didn't sound right. Every time she hit what she knew was the correct note, it sounded quite unlike Octavia knew it should! 'The notes just aren't sounding right,' said Mrs Lines, who was meant to be good at her job and know enough about pianos to tell when things weren't sounding as they should. The sounds that were coming from Fortepiano as Octavia tried in vain to get a proper tune going, were so bad, that after fifteen minutes Mrs Lines decided to abandon the lesson because, 'The piano just isn't sounding or working at all as it should.' Octavia was quite devastated. Her lovely piano – and well – something had gone badly wrong! Not only was Octavia very put out and upset, so was Fortepiano. He was quite unable to work out why his hammers were not working properly. It was all his fault, he thought. Now he would be sent back to the shop, maybe even the workshop! Oh the shame of it all! Just how could he bear it. He was, after all, a new piano and new pianos should work perfectly!

Chapter 9

After Octavia's disastrous piano lesson, Mr Brown immediately telephoned Mr Sharp in Edinburgh. He had sold the piano to Octavia's Grandmother and he delivered it. So he had to be the one to sort out Fortepiano's problem. After all his job was looking after pianos, keeping them tuned and in good order, so he was, if you like, a 'piano doctor'. Surely he'd be able to make Fortepiano better and able to play properly again. 'If Mr Sharp can't tell us what's wrong with your piano, then nobody can,' said Mr Brown to Octavia. She was quite beside herself with worry, and while her father was on the phone to Mr Sharp, had waited impatiently beside him. She wanted to try and hear what Mr Sharp was saying to her father, and she hoped that it wouldn't all be hopeless.

While all this was going on, Fortepiano stood in his corner feeling very sorry for himself. It was as if Octavia knew this too, for she had left her father talking to Mr Sharp and come to sit down on the piano stool. She patted Fortepiano's keys. 'Don't worry my beautiful piano, it will be all right, Mr Sharp will sort it out and then we can play nice tunes together again!' Fortepiano felt a bit better, Octavia wasn't going to send him back to the shop after all, he would be made to work properly again. Mr Brown had been right about Mr Sharp knowing what was wrong. 'It's a new piano,' he said. 'Things are bound to be a bit stiff and new, because the piano hasn't been played before. Don't worry, I'll be up in a few days and I'll come and take a look.' Now, by the time Mr Brown went back to Octavia in the sitting-room, she had again become rather upset about it all. She wasn't very hopeful at all now, and had begun to cry. She was wishing she had stayed to listen in to the call to Mr Sharp.

'Now, now, what's all this,' said her dad quite brightly. When Octavia looked at her dad through her tears she noticed he wasn't looking too serious about it all. 'It's going to be all right,' said Mr Brown. 'Mr Sharp will come and check your piano in a day or two, he'll sort it all out.' When Octavia heard this, she stopped crying. She was so relieved. Nothing ever is as bad as it seems, she thought to herself. And she went off to telephone Mrs Lines to tell her the news.

Of course Fortepiano was relieved too, everything was definitely not as bad as it seemed, he certainly agreed with Octavia about that!

Chapter 10

Fortepiano felt much better now, everything would turn out all right, as things normally did if you have patience. But a bit of him couldn't help wondering why his keys, when they had been working before, were not making the right sounds. Of course he just hadn't realised what was going on under his strings. It hadn't occurred to him that he had lodgers, and had been taken over in a big way by three naughty and very bored Triplets, who were, at this moment, sitting under his strings feeling very pleased with themselves for having, as they thought, put off Octavia's piano teacher. Only, what had they done to poor Octavia? They thought they had got one better on Mrs Lines, but really they had upset Octavia more than her teacher, because it was her piano they had been playing with! Their excuse was that they were bored. They had tried to behave, for during the first few minutes of Octavia's lesson they had sat quietly, listening. But they had decided they didn't like Mrs Lines very much, they weren't quite sure yet why, only they knew they had taken a dislike to her pink spectacle frames, which they thought made her eyes look like some strange insects' from the jungle! And of course they were very very bored of not playing any tricks for a long time. For it was this they were made for, or so they thought. It had been most definitely time to get up to some mischief, and while Octavia played her tunes to her teacher and did them very well, this gave them the idea, which mainly came from Poch, to push up the hammers on the opposite end from where Octavia was playing, so as she hit the correct notes, they made the hammers play the wrong ones! This resulted in a very unharmonious sound, and so this was why Octavia and Mrs Lines thought something had happened to Fortepiano.

The Triplets had had a super time! Now they were exhausted, and were sitting having a rest under Fortepiano's strings, but they were very pleased with their morning's mischief! 'That was good fun,' said Poco to the other two.

'I really enjoyed the sound we made,' replied Poch. 'Didn't you?'

'Yes,' shouted the other two.

'But,' said Placido hesitantly.

'But what?' said Poco.

'Well, I feel a tiny bit sorry for our Tendernote! We have upset her, not her teacher.'

'That can't be helped,' replied Poch in a very unconcerned voice. 'That pink-eyed lady,' for that's what the Triplets now called Mrs Lines, 'She deserved it, talking about "Triplets"! What does she know about us?' he went on.

'She seems to know quite a lot,' said Placido.

'Well she can't talk about us, if she doesn't know us,' said Poco. And they fell silent thinking about it all.

Of course Mrs Lines hadn't been talking about the Triplets at all, she had been explaining to Octavia how to count a rhythm in triplets! Which were three notes played in the time of two! But the Triplets weren't to know that!

As the Triplets had been talking, they had been moving their little heads up and down and back and forward. As they did this they were making Fortepiano's strings vibrate, and it was making him feel quite sick! What was happening to him, he thought. He must be ill after all, and maybe he did need the 'piano doctor'! There must be something wrong with me, my strings are making buzzing sounds. And he gave himself a huge shake, so much so that his three big legs wobbled very dangerously and the Triplets stopped talking and became very quiet, and a bit frightened, as they thought Fortepiano was going to collapse around them! 'Hold on tight!' shouted Poco, and they all grabbed one each of Fortepiano's strings with their hands. This made a kind of humming sound, so Fortepiano's legs began to shake even more, for he just couldn't understand what was happening to him. His legs were shaking, his strings were buzzing, and he felt sick and thoroughly fed up. It was going to be no good, his time was up, he was useless! And then, just when Fortepiano thought things couldn't become any worse, he thought he heard a voice coming from under his strings! He tried to stand very still, and not shake, so he could listen. There it was, he heard it again. This was all he needed, he was hearing voices as well as everything else!

Now the Triplets had been very frightened when Fortepiano had the 'wobbles', so, after thinking about this for a few minutes, they decided they had better speak up and let Fortepiano know they were there, and who they were. Poco had been elected as spokesperson and so as not to frighten Fortepiano and make his legs wobble again, he had spoken in what the Triplets called 'sotto voce', very quietly. This hadn't helped Fortepiano at all, as Poco had spoken so softly, Fortepiano had thought he was imagining voices! So Poco tried again. 'Fortepiano,' he whispered, a bit louder. 'Fortepiano, please don't be upset, but it's us, we're under here, under your strings!' Fortepiano nearly jumped right off his legs! He wasn't hearing voices, someone was really there!

'Who are you?' he asked. 'And however did you come to be under my strings?'

'Well,' said Poco, now popping up to show himself, 'we jumped! We had to, you see.' And then Poco went on to explain to Fortepiano just what had happened when they were in the piano workshop. And how, so they wouldn't be discovered, they had jumped inside Fortepiano, not really meaning to stay for long. 'We like it here,' said Poch.

'It's good fun,' said Placido.

Oh no, now Fortepiano was hearing, not one, but three voices!

'How many more of you are under there?' he asked.

'Only three,' said Poco.

'Yes, only the three of us,' echoed the other two. 'We're called Triplets,' they all said together. Fortepiano was amazed and a bit taken aback. They had been under his strings for ages, and he hadn't known! Then he had a thought. Wait a minute, all the times I've had my keys playing tunes, all the times I've thought I was magical and very special, it's been those three! Triplets, they call themselves. I'll give them Triplets! Then he had another quite terrible thought. If the Triplets had been doing all these things to him, playing his keys, making tunes sound wrong, then it must have been the Triplets who had messed up Octavia's lesson, and made her tunes sound wrong! Oh no, things had just taken a turn for the worse! The Triplets had by now become very quiet, and now Fortepiano too had become very quiet. The Triplets were quite un-nerved, he was so quiet. What would he do now, they wondered!

Chapter 11

The telephone was ringing. 'Answer it please Octavia,' shouted her mother. 'That might be Mr Sharp telling us when he's coming.' So Octavia dashed to the telephone; it was Mr Sharp, and he said he would be there to look at Octavia's piano that very day! Octavia was so relieved, now everything would be all right. Mr Sharp would find out what was wrong with Fortepiano, for, without thinking, Octavia had given her piano that name. Somehow she just knew that was the right name for him. If he had a name, then it made him more hers, which of course he was. Octavia hung around waiting for Mr Sharp to arrive. She wouldn't go anywhere, and even when her friends had called to take her out swimming with them, she excused herself, for how could she go anywhere until she knew Fortepiano would be fine!

'I hear a van coming,' called her mother from the kitchen, and sure enough, there was Mr Sharp at the front door with his black case in his hand looking just like a doctor! Well he was, sort of, thought Octavia, he was the piano doctor! By now Mrs Brown had come from the kitchen to let him in.

'Hi,' he said to Octavia and her mum. 'I hear you have a problem with your new piano?'

'Yes,' replied Octavia looking quite anxious, and she took him into the sitting-room. Fortepiano was still recovering from the shock of finding out about the Triplets. Now he had the added anguish of knowing that they had not only played a trick on him, but had played one on Octavia too! Maybe they didn't do it to her intentionally, but it had still happened, and now everyone thought something was wrong with him! Of course he knew there wasn't, and all his troubles were those Triplets, and now he was probably in for more trouble! What could he do about it all? Not much, he thought.

Everything had gone wrong, and he would have to try and work out if he could put it all right again. Just how he was going to do that would take a lot of thinking about. The problem was he didn't have much time to think because Octavia had just come into the room with the man who had delivered him to Octavia.

Now he was for it! And all because of those naughty Triplets. He would make them pay for this, oh yes he would . . .

Chapter 12

Octavia felt very apprehensive. What would Mr Sharp find? Would he maybe have to take Fortepiano back to Edinburgh? Oh she so hoped not. For then there would be no more piano lessons for her until Fortepiano was mended. 'Right,' said Mr Sharp to Octavia, 'off you go and find something to do, just let me get on with my job. I'll call you when I know what's wrong.' Octavia didn't want to leave the room, she wanted to stay beside Fortepiano.

'Come on,' said her mum, 'we'll go and have a drink of juice or coffee while we wait,' and she asked Mr Sharp if he would like a cup of coffee.

'Yes please,' he said. 'Black with no sugar please.' And Mrs Brown went off with Octavia, having to almost drag her out of the room. Octavia didn't want anything to drink, she was too upset and worried about what might be wrong with her piano. Not only that, she was thinking, but what would Grandma say when she found out, if there was something wrong! Mrs Brown saw how upset and worried Octavia was. 'It will be all right, nothing is ever as bad as it seems!' she said. Octavia sighed, she had heard that before, and she knew her mother was just trying to cheer her up. How did her mum know it wasn't going to get worse! When Mrs Brown had made the coffee for Mr Sharp she asked Octavia to take it in to him. This was just the chance she needed to get back into the sitting-room to see what was happening. She took the mug from her mum and went to the sitting-room door. I'd better knock first, she thought, just in case something terrible was happening to Fortepiano. So she gave a quick rap on the door and went in. Mr Sharp gave her a big smile, then he saw just how anxious Octavia was looking. 'It's OK Octavia, it is good news. Everything is working properly, there is nothing wrong with your piano.'

Well, Octavia was so relieved she gave a little jump in the air, and almost spilled all of Mr Sharp's coffee! He laughed. 'I think you'd better give me my mug of coffee before it's all gone!' So Octavia handed it to him, while thinking at the same time she must be going to be a terrible piano player! For if there was nothing wrong with Fortepiano, and she could make sounds like that when she played, then she thought I'm not going to be very good at playing the piano. She would have to practise even harder now, for she didn't want to hear those funny noises again at a lesson! Mr Sharp packed up his case with all his tools, and then, just as he was doing that, Mrs Brown came in to be told the good news. 'It's just new,' said Mr Sharp. 'Make sure you play it a lot Octavia, that will help.'

'Oh I will,' she replied.

Mr Sharp patted her on the head, and reminding her to keep practising, he went out of the room with Mrs Brown. 'There should be no big problems,' he told her. 'New pianos have to be played in.' And off he went, with a wave to Mrs Brown.

'There you are,' she said coming back into the room, 'I told you things wouldn't be as bad as they looked,' and she went off to do her ironing. But Octavia was just a tiny bit worried still. What if she couldn't play the piano and then it would be all nothing but a nice dream! She'd better start practising right now, after all it was the school holidays and she could practise more. So she sat down at her piano, opened her book, and began to play. Everything was fine, no more funny sounding notes and noises!

It's going to be all right, she thought as she played. But of course Fortepiano knew better; if anything, things were going to get a whole lot worse. Unless of course he could think of a way to stop the Triplets getting up to more mischief!

Chapter 13

While Mr Sharp had been in checking to see if there was anything wrong with Fortepiano, the Triplets had been very quiet, hiding in a space over to one side of Fortepiano's strings, where no one could find them. They had been listening very carefully to what was going on, hoping very much Mr Sharp wouldn't stay too long. He didn't of course, because there was nothing wrong with Fortepiano, nothing anyway that getting rid of the Triplets wouldn't cure! Mr Sharp wasn't to know of course, not being a specialist in musical little people. So, once he had gone, the Triplets came back out to their space under the strings. 'Phew,' said Poco, 'I'm glad he's gone!'

'Oh yes,' said the other two together.

'It would have been disaster all round if he had found us,' said Poch.

'Of course,' replied Placido, who was the one with the most brains, 'we could always have said the magic word to make us invisible, if the worst had come about.' If the Triplets were really in big trouble, that is, life-threatening, then they had a magic word which they could say to make them invisible. When they said the word 'accelerando', they vanished, but only for one beat of a minute!

'Yes, we know that,' said Poch. 'One problem solved, but we have still got the biggest problem,' and he stopped talking to think for a bit.

'Yes,' they all said together. 'We've now to face Fortepiano!'

'He looked very cross when he found out about us, and what we had done,' said Poco. And they all sat quietly again, as they did when they wanted to think over a problem that was very important. Fortepiano knew where they were now, and, at this very moment he was at his wits' end thinking about what the Triplets might do next! He knew he would always be blamed no matter what happened.

But what could he do, other than only hope Octavia wouldn't be upset again at a lesson! Fine chance that was going to be, because, as he knew now only too well, Triplets were easily bored. If only he could think of some plan to keep them amused while Octavia was having her lessons!

While Fortepiano was thinking about this problem, the Triplets were already onto their next mischievous idea, having become bored of thinking about how angry Fortepiano would be next time they popped up from his strings! What mischief could they do next? That was much more interesting than imagining how angry Fortepiano was, and much less frightening. For if they had thought about it carefully they would have realised things could become very nasty indeed, but mischief was their game, so they set to thinking up another plan! That was much better than thinking nasty thoughts.

Chapter 14

Today was Saturday again, Octavia's lesson day, and she was very excited. She had practised everything Mrs Lines had asked her to practise, and, she had even tried an extra page, so she hoped Mrs Lines would be pleased. She now knew all the names of the lines and spaces in both the treble and the bass clef, and all the little rhymes to help her remember them, and she knew the names of Fortepiano's keys. She did have a lot to remember, but she knew that if she learned it all properly, then she would be able to play lovely tunes. She was happy; everything had worked out, Fortepiano was fine, she had had all that worry for nothing! Her mother had been right of course, as mothers always are!

While Octavia, though, was deliriously happy, Fortepiano most definitely wasn't. For he knew today was Octavia's lesson day and he was beside himself with worry, in case the Triplets made him sound wrong again. And he still hadn't come up with any ideas that would distract them. He so wanted to help Octavia play well and get through her lesson with no interruptions. Then he had an idea. I know what I'll do, he thought to himself, if the Triplets come near my hammers again, I'll stop them with my dampers, then perhaps they won't make trouble! You see the dampers were little pads lined up in a row over Fortepiano's strings. If you pressed one of his pedals they all sat up off the strings, and that made the notes make a sound that lasted longer than normal. Since the Triplets lived most of the time under the strings, they would have to pass under the dampers if they wanted to reach the hammers, that hit the strings to make the sounds. The dampers, Fortepiano was thinking to himself, would act like a draw-bridge does on a castle.

A draw-bridge on a castle can be pulled up to keep the enemy out. The Triplets were sort of Fortepiano's enemies, and his dampers would act like a castle's draw-bridge. That's my plan of action then, he thought, that's what I'll do. It sounds all very complicated to someone who doesn't know much about the insides of pianos, but Fortepiano seemed to know what he was doing. He felt much better now that he had thought up his plan. He hoped it would work, but at the same time he hoped that he wouldn't need to put his plan into action; he hoped the Triplets would behave themselves! If not, then he felt better for coming up with a plan to save Octavia's lesson if the worst happened!

Chapter 15

Octavia's lesson was going well, she had played all the tunes Mrs Lines had given her to practise, she had even played the extra page she had practised too. 'You are doing very well,' said Mrs Lines. 'Soon you will be able to have a new book with proper tunes.' Up till now all Octavia's tunes had been only one or two lines. In between the tunes the book taught her all the things she needed to know to be able to play the piano properly. So now Octavia was looking forward to having a book with only tunes. If, she had to admit, there was a down side to learning the pian⌢, then it would be having to remember so much to begin with, and Mrs Lines had told her the piano was the most difficult instrument to play because you had to play hands together all the time and read two different clefs at once. 'And so,' said Mrs Lines, 'that is why the piano is called "the King of Instruments"!'

Well, when Fortepiano heard Mrs Lines say he was 'the King of Instruments,' he could barely stop his big legs wobbling with excitement! I'm a king, I'm a king! He kept saying over and over to himself. That means I am a very important person! Then he became very still on his three big legs while he thought about this momentous bit of news. This would most definitely have its advantages, he thought. Think of all the rules I can make, for Kings make rules, don't they? I will be able to make rules that will stop the Triplets doing awful things! Oh yes, this was definitely very good news for him. I will take action on my 'action', he thought. My 'action' is the most important bit of me, for this is the bits inside me that make the tunes when my keys are pressed. It's a bit like having a real heart, he thought. The Triplets had stopped his 'action' working properly, and that had caused him big trouble. Now he could maybe stop that happening again!

Maybe he could stop the Triplets misbehaving again during Octavia's lesson. He had found an answer to his problems, and Mrs Lines had unwittingly helped him. Help, he thought, often comes from the strangest people! Then he went back to listening to Octavia playing a tune on his keys.

Unfortunately he wasn't the only one who had heard Mrs Lines say he was the 'king of instruments', the Triplets had been listening to it all as well!

'This is going to be big trouble for us,' said Poco, and the other two nodded their little heads in agreement. 'There will be no stopping him now,' replied Poch, and the Triplets sat looking very worried, their little heads nodding up and down in time to the tune Octavia was playing, as they thought about how being the 'king of instruments' would change Fortepiano as far as they were concerned, and probably most definitely for the worse.

Chapter 16

Mrs Brown was on the telephone to the Music Shop in Inverness asking them to send Octavia her first proper tune book, and of course Octavia was very excited about it.

'It will be here in two days,' her mother told her. Octavia couldn't wait for it to arrive, for it would be here in time for Saturday's lesson, so she hoped Mrs Lines would give her her first tune from it then. She really didn't want to have to wait for another week, it was very important to Octavia because her Grandma and Grandpa would be arriving for a holiday soon, and she wanted to be able to play a proper tune, as she called it, to show them how well she was doing. So she went off to do her practice because she wanted to make sure she had everything right for Mrs Lines on Saturday. First of all she practised all her notes, then she played the tunes Mrs Lines had told her to prepare. Her favourite tune was called Secret Garden; in it her left hand had lots of chords to play, and she liked practising those because the chords made it sound very secret! She was quite pleased with what she had practised, so she then went over other tunes she had played before. She wanted to be quite sure Mrs Lines thought her good enough for a proper tune. Then she just sat there on the stool thinking how lucky she was to have such a kind Grandma who would give her such a beautiful piano. This is 'the King of Instruments', she thought, how good can it get to be playing 'the King of Instruments'!

Fortepiano was, at the same moment, thinking the same thing. He felt so important that he was nearly having another wobble again with excitement! Then Octavia came out of her dream and played another tune, and Fortepiano felt so proud of her. She looked after him so well.

She was always dusting him and cleaning him, and making his keys shine. 'Well, it's your piano, you have to look after it,' her mother had said. And Octavia was doing just that. Everything is so perfect, thought Fortepiano, well, almost everything. I've still got these Triplets and I'll never get rid of them, not unless I can find somewhere else for them to stay. And that made him start thinking about this problem again. His problem, the Triplets, who had been sitting quietly, and who were becoming restless again, had decided to go for a walk under Fortepiano's strings. Something might come up to amuse them, they thought. They walked around and as they looked up at the strings, they thought that they looked like a forest of bright gold wires shining in the sunlight, just waiting for somebody to have a swing on them! So that's what they did, had a walk around stopping occasionally to have a swing on one of the longer strings. As they did this a deep, low, stringy 'pop' came from each string. They were having such fun with their swinging, from one string to another they went, right from one end of Fortepiano to the other! For three little people that was a long way, because Fortepiano had over two hundred of them. When they got to the other end they flopped down onto the wood. 'Phew!' they all said at once, 'that was good fun!'

Now of course, all this 'swinging' hadn't gone un-noticed by Fortepiano, because every time the Triplets swung on a string, it vibrated, and this became very annoying for him. A piano doesn't like having his strings used as a 'swing park'. They're very important, a piano's strings! For when the hammers hit them, then you get the different sounds. So, Fortepiano was NOT amused! 'Go away,' he said, but the Triplets had been having such a good time, they hadn't heard him.

When they had exhausted themselves, he was very relieved. At last, they have tired themselves out, there will be no more trouble today! But of course not many moments later he was to be proved wrong, and not only that, Octavia was still sitting there! Would she notice, or had she noticed already something wasn't quite as it should be? Time would tell.

Chapter 17

Octavia had noticed that something was wrong with Fortepiano. As she had been playing, the Triplets had been swinging on the strings! And Octavia was hearing a strange vibrating sound as she hit the keys! Here we go again, thought Fortepiano, trouble always comes in threes! This time Octavia tried very hard not to panic or become upset. Mr Sharp told me my piano was working perfectly, she thought to herself, so there must be another logical explanation. It must be my playing, I'm not going to be a very good pianist after all! And I'll never make the Albert Hall or Young Musician of the Year if when I am playing it sounds as awful as this!

Fortepiano was trying to stand very still on his three big legs, and not make them shake, for he was horrified that Octavia thought her piano playing wasn't good enough! Of course it was good enough, she didn't know about the Triplets. He couldn't make up his mind if that was a good thing or a bad thing. The Triplets swinging on his strings was guaranteed to put Octavia's playing off. He had been so busy worrying about what damage the Triplets were doing to his strings, he had quite forgotten Octavia was still practising! Now she was becoming upset again because she had heard the strange sounds herself coming from his strings. What could he do – nothing really – for he was when it came down to it – a piano – he was quite helpless!

Octavia just sat there too terrified this time to go to her Mum and Dad for they would just call Mr Sharp again! Oh dear, what am I going to do, she thought. Maybe if I just try my tune one more time – maybe I have imagined it all! So she opened her book again at one of her tunes – and wouldn't you know it – the notes sounded just fine! She had been imagining it, she thought; after all she didn't know enough about pianos yet to know what sounded right or wrong, so maybe she had played a few wrong notes, and that was what made her think the piano had gone wrong again. Feeling a lot happier about things she finished playing and closed her book, giving a big sigh of relief. There was nothing wrong – and she would be able to have her lesson on Saturday as usual.

Off she went out of the room happily humming one of her tunes to herself.

Of course Fortepiano knew differently – but was quite thankful that Octavia was off happy again.

Chapter 18

Weeks were passing when all Fortepiano had to put up with was the Triplets using his strings as a swing park! It almost seemed as if they had forgotten about Octavia and Mrs Lines! Fortepiano was beginning to relax a little about it all. Maybe having the Triplets live with him wasn't going to be as bad as he thought. He could just about cope with having his strings pinged and vibrated if the Triplets didn't do anything more to upset his dear Octavia. But of course the Triplets, if only Fortepiano had known it, had other ideas! They were so bored with trying to behave all the time, and since Octavia's first lesson, had ignored Octavia and Mrs Lines at lesson time on Saturday mornings. But this particular Saturday they couldn't behave themselves any more.

Octavia was learning a tune from her new book, it was to be a surprise for Grandma and Grandpa, who were to arrive the next day. She had been practising hard at getting it just right, and she hoped Mrs Lines would say it was good enough to play to Grandma and Grandpa. 'It's coming on very nicely,' said Mrs Lines after Octavia had played it to her.

The tune was a 'Minuet', which was a stately dance, and Octavia had tried very hard to play it at the correct speed. But Mrs Lines decided that it wasn't sounding quite right. She decided to play the tune to Octavia herself to show her the correct way to play it. So Octavia got up from the piano stool to let Mrs Lines sit down to play. This should be interesting, thought Fortepiano, for he had never heard Mrs Lines play before; neither had Octavia, and more to the point the Triplets hadn't heard her play either!

'It's that woman playing who is meant to be teaching Octavia. Remember she was talking about us a while back,' said Poco.

'So it is,' answered Poch and Placido together. They had all remembered the day they had heard Mrs Lines talking about 'triplets' to Octavia, and had thought she was talking about them! They had been very angry. Now they could maybe get their revenge – big time! Fortepiano felt his strings vibrate as the Triplets became more and more worked up and excited. Oh no, now we're in for trouble he thought.

The Triplets had decided that since it was Mrs Lines who was playing, they would go into action. As Mrs Lines hit a key it made a little hammer pop up and hit a string, then you got the nice sounds. As she was hitting the keys the Triplets grabbed each hammer as it came up to stop it hitting the strings, so no sound came out! Mrs Lines was very puzzled at what was happening. Every time she hit a key there was no sound. She kept trying again and again, but it was no use, she just couldn't play the tune properly for Octavia! She was gradually becoming very impatient and very angry. Poor Octavia could only sit very still, completely mystified at what was happening, for it only seemed a second ago when she had played the tune that the keys were working! Octavia had thought the Minuet had sounded fine, all the notes sounded correct to her. So what had happened, whatever was the matter with Fortepiano now, she thought.

'This is quite ridiculous,' said Mrs Lines crossly and she stopped trying to play the tune. 'This piano is no good, it doesn't work properly!' Octavia began to cry, whatever was she going to do, now her Grandma wouldn't hear her play, and she would ask Mr Sharp to take her piano away! This, as far as Octavia was concerned, was the end of all her dreams!

Mrs Lines, who was by now absolutely furious, got up from the piano stool, picked up her music case, and stormed out the sitting-room, up the hall and out of the front door, banging it as she went! There was so much noise that Mr and Mrs Brown came running into the hall to find out what was happening, and then into the sitting-room.

'It's my piano,' sobbed Octavia, who was by now in a terrible state. 'Mrs Lines was playing it and it sounded all wrong again, and she is very angry,' wailed Octavia, crying even harder.

'Oh dear me,' said Octavia's Dad and Mum at once. 'Whatever can the problem be now?' said Mr Brown.

'I don't know,' shouted Octavia, getting very worked up. 'But if you don't do something I am going to have no piano and no music teacher!' By now Octavia was quite hysterical.

'It can't be that bad,' Mrs Brown was saying. 'Mr Sharp said the piano was fine.'

'Yes,' replied Octavia's father. 'It is just because your piano is new, and Mrs Lines should understand that too!'

'I don't care what anyone says,' shouted Octavia again, 'I just want my piano to work properly!'

'Now, now, dear,' said her mother as she patted her on the back, 'I'm sure your piano will be fine, why don't you play something for us, then your dad and I can hear for ourselves what's wrong.'

So Octavia, who was by now alternating between crying and feeling cross, sat down on the stool and began to play her tune, not before she had told her parents that it was stupid asking her to play if the piano wouldn't work! 'It won't play you know, you'll just have to phone Mr Sharp again!'

While all this drama was going on Fortepiano had become almost demented, for he knew exactly what the trouble was, and so did the Triplets who by now had run for cover as far away inside Fortepiano as possible!

These three, thought Fortepiano, have ruined everything for Octavia this time, well almost everything! And he stood there feeling very annoyed with the Triplets. He was now anxiously waiting for Octavia's reaction, and that of her parents, when Octavia began to play him again. He knew his keys would play properly now the Triplets had gone away into hiding! And of course he played quite beautifully. Whenever Octavia began to play her tune Fortepiano's keys were working, in fact the tune sounded really nice. 'Why,' said Mr Brown, 'that is really very good playing Octavia!'

'Yes,' said her mother. 'However could Mrs Lines have thought there was anything wrong!' And both parents looked at each other and Octavia completely mystified.

'But it wasn't sounding right,' said Octavia. 'I heard it too!'

'Well it's fine now,' her father replied. Then both her parents left Octavia to her practising, Mr Brown going off to phone Mrs Lines to try and calm her down and make sure she would give Octavia piano lessons again, although neither parents were very hopeful of that. And Fortepiano as well as the Triplets were quite pleased when they heard she might not return, as there was something really odd, they thought, about her. She was quite frightening when she was angry, she looked just like a witch!

Chapter 19

The next day Octavia was exhausted after all the drama of the day before. She hadn't slept well either, for she had kept thinking of what would happen if she started playing her tune to Grandma and the funny sounds started again! She had been so worried that she had got up very early the next morning to practise, and to check that Fortepiano was working properly. Of course I am playing properly, I always do, thought Fortepiano. He was feeling quite grumpy that people, in particular Mrs Lines, were thinking he wasn't a good piano. Of course he was one of the very best, it just showed what Mrs Lines knew about pianos! He felt that it just wasn't good enough that he had to take all the blame for the Triplets' bad behaviour. Well, he was thinking, today had to be perfect, this was Octavia's big day, her grandparents were arriving, and she would play them the tune she had been learning. Nobody must blame him today of all days! But then he had another quite horrible thought, would the Triplets know Octavia was playing to her grandparents? Did they pay much attention to who Octavia was playing to? That was definitely a problem. Oh, it was so annoying not knowing what they were up to all the time under his strings! After he had this thought, he became more and more nervous. But Fortepiano wasn't the only nervous person in the Brown household.

Octavia was also beside herself with nerves and excitement. She couldn't decide which was worse. 'Oh do stop worrying,' said her mother. 'Granny and Grandpa will love your playing. You have learned very hard to play and you do it very well.'

'Yes,' said Mr Brown, 'you have practised very hard.'

They were all in the sitting-room waiting for Octavia's grandparents to arrive.

They were coming all the way from Edinburgh by car; Octavia knew it was a long and tiring journey, but she hoped they wouldn't be too tired to listen to her playing her tune, for she didn't think she could wait until the next day!

Fortepiano stood in his corner, looking, he thought, quite splendid! Octavia had given him a special dust and polish that morning, so he knew his wood was shining and his keys were gleaming white. He just hoped that he would sound good too! No Triplet problems today he hoped.

Octavia's thoughts, if she had known, were in accord with Fortepiano's. This was, as far as she was concerned, her big day. It was important for her to play really well for her Grandparents, nothing must go wrong!

There it was! The sound of a car, they had arrived! Mr and Mrs Brown, Octavia and the two dogs all went to the door to meet Granny and Grandpa. There were hugs all round and pats on the head for Jazz and Storm. Mr Brown helped Grandpa in with the cases while Octavia and her mum took Granny upstairs to her room. 'Just take your time and settle in,' said Octavia's mum. 'Dinner will be in half an hour. Come on Octavia, you can help me set the table while

Granny and Grandpa get settled.' So Octavia had to follow her mum downstairs to the kitchen, and she hadn't even been able to say anything about her tune to Granny; well never mind, all that mattered was they had arrived at last!

Chapter 20

At last! Octavia couldn't wait! Her dad and mum and granny and grandpa had sat down round the sitting-room fire after dinner with their mugs of coffee. Everyone was talking, catching up on all the news, but Octavia wasn't really listening to any of it, she was thinking about playing her tune. Would she be able to play it correctly, and more importantly, would the piano sound good!

'Octavia,' said her grandma. Octavia jumped. 'You weren't listening Octavia, we were asking if you were ready to play to us?' Well of course she was, she had been waiting for ages to be asked. Now the time had arrived, she felt very nervous. She went and sat down on the piano stool, opened her book, placed her fingers on the keys, took a big breath, then began to play her tune. When she finished there was just a silence in the room. Octavia couldn't take a breath herself as she waited for someone to say something. 'Oh very well played,' shouted Grandma and Grandpa together, and then everyone began to clap. Octavia could breath again! She had done it! And everyone, especially Grandma, had liked her playing,

now she could relax. Nothing had gone wrong, even Fortepiano had behaved himself!

'You play well, and have learned it all very quickly,' said
Grandma. 'The piano sounds very good, just as it did when
I played it in the shop!'

Wait a minute, thought Octavia, Grandma played it.
Grandma must be able to play the piano too. 'Grandma,' she
asked, 'can you really play the piano too?'

Before Grandma could reply, Grandpa said, 'Grandma
used to teach the piano, and before that she did a bit of
performing at concerts too, she was very good.'

Well, Octavia was speechless. 'Where,' she asked, 'did
Grandma play at concerts?'

'In the Usher Hall in Edinburgh, that was just one of the
places. She played at the Albert Hall in London and lots of
places around the world! It would take a long time to tell you
all the famous places grandma played at, that was before she
met me,' and he laughed. 'Then she couldn't travel so much
anymore so she taught boys and girls like you, she was a very
good pianist,' said Grandpa.

'Oh be quiet,' said Grandma, looking quite embarrassed.
Wow, thought Octavia, her Grandma had played in all the
famous places she had dreamed of playing at, and no one had
told her!

'Grandma, that's wonderful,' replied Octavia. 'It's a pity
you live so far away, you could have taught me!'

'Oh it was a long time ago,' said Grandma, and she smiled
at Octavia. 'My fingers are too stiff now to play much, but I
hope that you will practise hard, then maybe some day you
might get to play in a famous concert hall in front of a big
audience too.'

'Oh I hope so, I'd really like to,' said Octavia, and she
went off again into one of her dreams, thinking about it all
again.

'Time for bed Octavia, you've had a long and exciting day,' said her mother. And for once Octavia didn't want to argue with her mother about going to bed, for she felt very tired, and wanted to go to bed, for then she could think about Grandma playing the piano in big concert halls, and dream of how she might be able to do the same one day. So she said goodnight to everyone and then off she went quite happily to bed to dream big dreams!

Chapter 21

Grandma and Grandpa stayed a whole fortnight, and during that time Octavia played lots of tunes to Grandma, sometimes Grandma just sat and listened, sometimes she gave Octavia advice about her playing. During all this Fortepiano sounded very good, and he felt very pleased with himself as he stood in his corner looking shiny and new. The Triplets also stayed out of the way and were very quiet and well behaved. The reason for their good behaviour? Well, they were frightened of Grandma, and slightly in awe of her, for, to them, she was a top 'virtuoso', and you don't annoy top virtuosos! So, all in all, the fortnight that Grandma and Grandpa were staying everything had gone very well. Octavia was pleased with her playing and very pleased that nothing had gone wrong with Fortepiano.

Now Octavia and her dad and mum were standing at the door waving to Grandma and Grandpa as they left on their drive back to Edinburgh. Octavia felt quite sad, she would miss them. She had learned a lot from Grandma, probably more than she had learned in her short time with Mrs Lines!

'Don't be sad,' said her mother, 'they will be back again soon,' and with that happy thought in her head Octavia went off to practise for her next lesson, that is if Mrs Lines was coming back!

Fortepiano was happy too, Grandma had been pleased with him! And miracle of miracles! The Triplets hadn't caused any trouble. Life was good, maybe the Triplets were going to live happily with him after all!

Chapter 22

Poco, Poch, and Placido had been quiet and well behaved now for too long, but of course that was only because Octavia's grandmother had been there. But Grandma was away now, and they were restless and bored, and ready for mischief! Using Fortepiano's strings as a swing park was fine but that got boring after a while. And the Triplets needed something new and exciting to do!

It was Saturday morning again, which meant it was Octavia's lesson day, and that meant a visit from Mrs Lines who had very nearly refused to come back and teach Octavia after the last disastrous lesson a few weeks ago when the Triplets had stopped Fortepiano's keys from sounding right, so Mrs Lines couldn't play Octavia's Minuet to her. Today, on this Saturday morning, the Triplets had been awake and moving about under Fortepiano's strings for hours. What were they up to now? Fortepiano could feel the Triplets were restless, for they were walking around a lot under his strings and everywhere else. He was sure his sounding board, that was the wood under his strings, would be quite worn out soon! And he was becoming worried again as he knew it was lesson day. Had, he wondered, the Triplets forgotten about Mrs Lines; he wasn't so sure. He hoped the lesson would go well and the Triplets would ignore her, but as far as Fortepiano was concerned that was only a nice dream, for the naughty Triplets were planning their 'big comeback' and it had to do with their most unfavourite person, Mrs Lines. They had definitely not forgotten about her!

'Right you two,' said Poch, 'I have an idea that will stop that teacher from talking about us anymore.' The Triplets were still sure that Mrs Lines had been saying horrible things about them to Octavia.

After all they had heard their name being mentioned by her at one of Octavia's lessons! Or so they thought. And even Triplets knew that it wasn't nice to talk about people behind their backs!

'I hope it's a good idea,' Poco replied.

'Oh yes, it's the best one I've had yet!' answered Poch.

'Mmm,' said Placido, 'time will tell!'

'Well, come on then tell us what your plan is,' said Poco. For if the truth were told he was becoming a bit fed up with Poch's ideas, he didn't think that up to now they were exciting enough. So Poch began to explain to the other two his new plans for their 'big comeback', and of course that meant another harassing lesson for Mrs Lines. Fortepiano had been listening to all of their conversation very carefully, and didn't at all like what he was hearing. Now there was definitely going to be big trouble, and he most definitely would be taking the blame once again. There must be something he could do . . .

Chapter 23

This wasn't going to be easy, thought Poco to himself. It all sounded rather complicated, this plan of Poch's. The last time they had stopped Fortepiano's hammers from hitting the strings it had only been some of the hammers they had stopped. Now Poch wanted to stop all of them from working! This was a big thir.g to do, for Poco knew that if they did it, then no notes would play! Poch had told them they would climb down to where Fortepiano's hammers were, they were going to go all the way down and this was quite tricky as they had to squeeze first under the dampers, slide off the sounding board, and then go right between each hammer! 'This,' said Poch, 'is going to be the tricky bit, because there's no space really down there at all.' It was going to be a tight fit, even for three tiny little Triplets. Then Poch told them if they couldn't stop every hammer, then they would have to stop every second one instead, a bit like when they did it before.

'Too complicated,' both Poco and Placido said at once.

'It can't be done,' said Placido.

'I agree,' replied Poco with some relief that Placido wasn't happy about it either.

'Nonsense,' answered Poch. 'We did it before and it worked, just take the last time as a trial run.'

But the other two were still not terribly convinced. 'What if we get stuck,' said Placido. 'Then we will really be in trouble.'

'Yes, and if Fortepiano can't play anymore we will have to go back with him to the workshop!' replied Poco. 'And we don't want to go back there!'

'I agree,' said Placido. 'It's much nicer here, than living in an old metronome!'

Poch set about trying to reassure them it wouldn't come to that, because he felt he had planned it all out properly. 'Now we have the idea we'll make it work,' he said.

'We've got the idea,' shouted Placido very loudly. 'It's your idea, not ours!' Poco was quite scared when Placido shouted at Poch, because Placido was the quietest of the three. He must be very worked up to shout like that, thought Poco. But Poch was not put off his plan, and so the other two had to sit quietly and pretend to listen as Poch gave out his instructions.

Fortepiano had only heard snatches of the Triplets' conversation, but it was enough to know by their excited voices that something big was about to happen, and there was no ignoring the fact Fortepiano was involved, he couldn't not be, for it was his insides that the Triplets were talking about! In not many hours' time it would all be over; he would be sent back to the shop or workshop to find out what was wrong with him. Only they would find there was nothing wrong at all! The only good thing was, he thought, the Triplets would end up back there too, back to living in their old metronome! What a terrible ending to what could have been a wonderful time. His legs trembled at the thought of it all. What would happen now?! He just found it all too much to think about and too horrifying to imagine!

Chapter 24

Octavia was hurrying, she had slept in and her mother had just wakened her. She had finished washing her face, cleaning her teeth and tidying her hair when the front doorbell rang! It must be Mrs Lines, surely she wasn't that late and it was her lesson time already! She hurried off downstairs to open the door, but her mother had got to the door before her. 'Good morning, it's a nice morning,' said Octavia's mother to Mrs Lines.

'Mmm,' replied Mrs Lines, 'I hope it's going to be a nice morning!'

Octavia stopped rather quickly at the bottom of the stairs when she heard Mrs Lines' cross voice. Her father had persuaded her teacher that everything was back to normal with the piano, but Mrs Lines didn't look too pleased this morning, she had definitely been put off by Fortepiano and the strange sounds coming from him at the last lesson. Oh well, thought Octavia, I'll have to do my very best playing to cheer her up! Mrs Lines went into the sitting-room followed by Octavia, her mother had gone back to the kitchen, and wasn't very happy with the way Mrs Lines had greeted her. She hoped that Octavia's lesson would go well, for she hadn't even said hello to her. Octavia had noticed this too, that's a bit rude, Octavia thought. Mrs Lines sat down on the stool beside the piano and Octavia went and sat down on the piano stool, quietly waiting for Mrs Lines to say something. 'I'd like you to play your scales first,' she said straight out, ignoring Octavia's look of surprise at her rudeness. Octavia decided to ignore Mrs Lines and her bad mood and proceeded to play her first scale. She was far enough on now to be learning scales and she very much wanted to sit her first piano exam, and for this she had to learn to play scales as well as tunes. Octavia wanted to do well in her exam.

She had been practising very hard at everything with a lot of help from Grandma when she had been staying. Everything Mrs Lines asked her to do, she thought she had done quite well, but Mrs Lines made no comment about how well she had played everything, she just said 'I don't think you have been practising enough!' Then she went on 'I expect a high standard from my pupils!'

Well, of course Octavia had been practising, every day for an hour, sometimes more. How could Mrs Lines be so nasty! Octavia felt she had to stand up for herself, so she told Mrs Lines just how hard she had been practising, and of how Grandma had helped her too.

'Well it doesn't sound like it to me,' said Mrs Lines. 'What does your Grandma know about playing the piano; nothing, you will have to put in more practice!' Well, now, thought Octavia, that was very rude making comments about Grandma like that, what does she know about Grandma?! But instead of being cheeky back Octavia just listened quietly to what Mrs Lines was saying; she was the teacher after all and Octavia was polite enough to know you don't argue or speak back to your teacher!

While Mrs Lines was giving Octavia a 'pep-talk' the Triplets were very carefully making their way across Fortepiano to carry out their plan. They had been listening to what Mrs Lines was saying to Octavia and this had made them more determined to do something. Of course Poch had realised – not that he had mentioned it to the others – that they might not be able to carry out the plan when they arrived, because Mrs Lines might not play a note! Especially now she was so cross. Poco and Placido hadn't thought of this, if they had, they would have been even more against his plan than they were, and wouldn't have gone at all. So Poch kept this bit of information to himself. He had made up his mind he would go for Plan B if Plan A didn't work. You see he had it all worked out. The other two had quite misjudged him. They always thought he didn't think things through, which you must do if you want your plan to work well. And it looked as if, this morning, his idea might work, at least that was as far as the Triplets were concerned. For once Mrs Lines had finished her 'pep-talk' she had decided to play to Octavia the tune she had given her to practise, and which she said Octavia hadn't practised enough! Mrs Lines changed stools with Octavia and before she began to play told Octavia to make sure she was listening properly and following the music.

While this had all been going on the Triplets had arrived at their destination inside Fortepiano, and with a lot of squeezing and pushing, had managed to push themselves under the little wooden hammers, not between them as Poch had told them to do. They had only realised they could do this when they got there, for they found there was space after all. That's just typical, though Poco, Poch hasn't worked it out properly after all! Well they were there now and Poco hoped it would be worth all the squeezing and pushing they were doing!

Of course Fortepiano didn't hope anything like that for he knew Mrs Lines was about to play, and as far as he was concerned it was going to be the end of a lovely partnership!

Chapter 25

When Mrs Lines began playing it took Fortepiano all his strength to keep his three big legs from wobbling with fright! What, he was thinking to himself, was going to happen? Nothing very good; that, he was very certain of.

Poco, Poch, and Placido were waiting patiently, just a few more notes, thought Poch to himself, then we can start! Octavia was listening very carefully to the music and to how Mrs Lines was playing it, she was concentrating so hard she missed the first signs that some of the notes weren't sounding right, but then she began to realise notes were not sounding or working as they should. For, as Mrs Lines was hitting the keys, she had to hit them harder and harder to get a sound! Every time she went to hit a key she had to lift her fingers higher and hit it very hard, but nothing seemed to help, and her face at first was looking puzzled, but then she began to turn a very funny purple colour as she got crosser and crosser! She was half way through playing the tune to Octavia when it had started sounding wrong, now she just couldn't seem to get a proper sound at all. One key when she pressed it would play, then another one wouldn't. It was almost as if, thought Octavia, someone was trying to stop any sound coming from the piano at all, but this wasn't possible, she thought.

The Triplets were having a great time, they had spread themselves out the length of Fortepiano's keys, and that was a big distance for three little people like them, because Fortepiano had eighty-eight white and black notes with hammers for them all. Poco was at one end, Poch was in the middle, and Placido was at the other end. So whenever Mrs Lines hit a key one of them would stop the hammer from hitting the string by holding on to it!

They were thoroughly enjoying themselves. Mrs Lines wouldn't be talking about 'Triplets' anymore, they thought, not after this. This would teach her a lesson. It was going very well for the Triplets but of course it was going very badly for Mrs Lines and Octavia. Fortepiano? Well he was in a terrible state. He was being pulled, clicked, pinged, and hit so hard, he didn't know how much longer he could stand it! How could they, he thought, how could they ruin it all for me and hurt me so much. His insides hurt so much he was sure his legs would shake so badly they would fall off! Octavia was at that very moment thinking along the same lines as Fortepiano, but of course she didn't know what Fortepiano knew, that there were little people making his insides go all over the place! It's happening again, it's my worst nightmare, she was thinking. Then her thoughts were interrupted by a loud bang! Mrs Lines had done the unthinkable, she had banged Fortepiano's lid down she was so cross! She crashed it down so hard that it made Fortepiano's legs give a terrible wobble and the Triplets got such a fright they all fell backwards inside Fortepiano!

'That's it!' Mrs Lines shouted, by now looking very purple and red with rage. 'Enough is enough! If you wish to continue lessons with me Octavia, you will have to come to my house; I will not teach on such a useless, tuneless, feeble sounding piano anymore. King of Instruments – more like a tramp!!' When Fortepiano heard all this he was horrified! Mrs Lines had called him names, she had called him a 'tramp'! Oh dear, he thought, how much worse would it get. Calling names wasn't a nice thing to do, especially coming from a piano teacher.

By now Mrs Lines had picked up her music case and once again stamped out of the sitting-room, and then, changing her mind, she came back in. 'And what is more,' she continued, just as if she had never stopped talking, 'if you wish to continue with me as your teacher, then get another piano!' And this time she left the room and went off out the front door banging it very loudly as she went, without even a goodbye! Octavia was left standing beside Fortepiano quite speechless with shock. Fortepiano himself stood in his corner trying very hard to keep his big legs from shaking, while the Triplets, who had been listening to it all as well, crawled back under Fortepiano's strings trying hard not to make any noise or jiggle Fortepiano's strings. Octavia had to sit down on the stool her legs were shaking so badly. What on earth had just happened, she was thinking. But of course she knew, she had seen it all and heard it. The keys had been working, making lovely sounds, then, they hadn't! Mr Sharp said there was nothing wrong with her piano, so what was going on, she was more puzzled now than upset.

Then her mother came into the room to find out what all the noise and banging had been about. 'She's not off again!' she said, meaning Mrs Lines. 'Whatever's the matter now, what's happened to make her so cross this time Octavia?'

Now Octavia had to explain to her mother what had just happened at her lesson. So she tried to explain, without crying or becoming too upset about it all, she was trying to be grown up about it, and not make it seem as bad as she felt it was, as you do sometimes when things go wrong. 'I can't quite understand it,' Mrs Brown was saying. 'It looks as if we will have to get your father to phone Mr Sharp again; he will begin to think we are becoming a nuisance!'

Octavia thought about what her mother was saying for a moment. 'Perhaps if I just try playing a tune myself we might be able to hear what is the matter, then we will be able to explain properly to Mr Sharp what is happening,' she said, trying to be very grown up about it.

'Good idea,' replied her mother, for she was by now feeling embarrassed and worried about it all. Not only would they maybe have to phone Mr Sharp, but it was looking very much as if they were going to have to look for a new piano teacher as well! So with all this going round in Mrs Brown's head she urged Octavia to try playing the piano one more time. Octavia sat down and opened her book to the same tune Mrs Lines had been playing. Now we're for it, thought Fortepiano, get yourselves out of this mess my little Triplet friends! But Octavia didn't get to play her tune, for just as she was about to play the door bell rang and Mrs Brown went off to answer it, and to let in all of Octavia's friends who had come to see her. They all rushed into the sitting-room, and so Octavia was quite distracted by all the noise and talking. They were all talking to Octavia at once and there was so much noise that Octavia forgot for the moment her troubles with Fortepiano, and went with her friends upstairs to her bedroom for a chat. In a way Fortepiano was quite glad, because what would happen if or when Octavia found out that there was nothing wrong with him!

Mrs Brown was also quite glad Octavia had been distracted because if Mrs Brown were to be honest she had her own thoughts about the problem of Fortepiano and Mrs Lines.

Maybe, she was thinking to herself, maybe Mrs Lines wasn't such a good teacher or player as she made out. Then she remembered the saying which she thought was quite true, 'a bad workman always blames his tools!'

Chapter 26

It was the middle of the night and Octavia had wakened up with a jump, as you sometimes do when you are in a deep sleep and a worrying thought wakens you up. What, she thought, had wakened her – then she remembered – her music lesson and the disaster it had ended up in! Mrs Lines had gone giving her an ultimatum, either go to her house for lessons, which she definitely didn't want to do, or get another piano, which she wasn't even going to consider. But what could she do about the mess? Then she remembered that her friends had arrived just as she was about to play her tune to try and find out what was wrong with Fortepiano, and horror of horrors, they had taken her mind off her piano problem so much she hadn't yet gone back to try and play her tune again, to see if she could find out what had happened to her piano when Mrs Lines was playing. That was what must have wakened her, she was worrying about it even when she was sleeping! Then, when she had rubbed all the sleep from her eyes, she made up her mind what she would do. Because it was the middle of summer, it was quite light outside even though it was the early hours of the morning. This meant she could go downstairs right now and check on Fortepiano. She wouldn't need any lights on so maybe if she was very quiet she wouldn't wake her parents. She looked at her bedside clock. It was four o'clock in the morning, she would have to be very quiet if she didn't want to waken her parents. She got out of bed, put on her dressing gown, and tiptoed very quietly downstairs to the sitting-room. Fortepiano was very surprised when he saw Octavia coming into the room. She must be very worried to come down to the sitting-room in the middle of the night, he thought.

Octavia sat down on the piano stool, laid her hands on the keys, gave a big sigh, and began, as quietly as she could to play her tune. She was concentrating so hard on her playing she had played quite a lot of her tune before she realised that her piano was sounding just as it should; I thought so, there is nothing wrong with my piano, she said to herself. Then she sat there on the stool puzzling over how then the piano hadn't sounded at all right when Mrs Lines had played it, she had heard it too, it had almost sounded as if the keys were playing on their own, it was almost as if they were deciding themselves when to make a sound or not! But, she thought, they couldn't, could they, they are just piano keys, piano keys can't play on their own! As she was puzzling over all this she had leant on the top of Fortepiano's lid with her head on her hands, and promptly fell asleep thinking about it all!

Fortepiano felt very sorry for Octavia; she had been worrying over nothing, and now the poor child was so tired she had fallen asleep right there on his lid. He would have to be very still and quiet so as not to waken her; he just hoped those Triplets would be doing the same!

Chapter 27

By now Fortepiano was very angry with the Triplets, they had caused so much trouble, and for what purpose, there was none he could think of, they only wanted to make mischief! Octavia was so worried she hadn't been able to sleep and had come down in the middle of the night, and now she had fallen asleep right there on his lid! He had to do something because who knew what the morning would bring? Maybe Mr Brown making a phone call to Mr Sharp, and maybe Fortepiano being exchanged for another piano! That was quite unthinkable, he knew he was a very good piano. There was no need to take him back to Edinburgh, if anyone should be removed back to Edinburgh it was the Triplets! But of course the worst of it was they couldn't go without him! There was only one thing left to do, he would have to have a serious talk with them.

The Triplets knew they were in big trouble, so much so that they were hiding right down under the lowest of Fortepiano's strings! They didn't really care too much though, they were made for making 'musical mischief' – they were the Triplets! At this precise moment though they weren't feeling too good, for they cruld feel Fortepiano's legs were shaking, in fact all of him was shaking! He must be very angry with us, they were thinking, and not only that, as they looked up and over to the front of Fortepiano they were horrified to see the little 'Tendernote' asleep on Fortepiano's lid! Placido actually felt quite sorry for her, but the other two could only think about how they had finally got Mrs Lines in a state and she had left. They felt she wasn't really as good a teacher or player as she made out. They weren't completely silly and stupid, they could tell a good pianist when they heard one!

In fact they thought they had done Octavia a favour, but how to explain this to Fortepiano was the problem, he was probably too angry now to listen to them. But maybe there was something else they could try. It was Poco who thought of it first. Looking at the other two who were trying to think their way out of the mess he said, 'Why don't we try and explain what we did to the little "Tendernote", she might listen to us?'

'Don't be stupid,' Poch replied. 'We're not meant to show ourselves to humans, we don't want anyone from the human world to know we are here.'

Poco was annoyed at his idea being turned down. 'It was only an idea,' he said feeling a bit let down. Then, much to Poco's surprise, Placido said it was the best idea yet. Poch then had to agree. 'Well, it might work, I suppose it's worth a try, it might save us from being put out.' Poch knew none of them wanted that because they liked it where they were.

'Let's do it then,' Placido said. So they all stood up feeling very nervous. They didn't really know what they were going to say, and anyway how would Octavia react when she heard them speak to her, they might frighten her even more! But they had to try this, otherwise Fortepiano and themselves would be back in the shop in Edinburgh before they knew it, or so they thought!

Chapter 28

As the Triplets arrived near to where Octavia was sitting she was still sound asleep and dreaming that there were three small people standing in front of her. She could see them quite clearly, they were all dressed the same in black and white with little black flat hats on their heads, they looked just like piano keys she thought. All three were waving their little hands at her, they seemed to be trying to get her attention, not realising at first she was sleeping. Who were they? She tried to lift her hand to wave back but her hand felt so heavy and she felt so tired . . .

Poco, Poch, and Placido were now standing lined up along the top of the piano lid looking down on Octavia, they were trying to speak to her, at least that's what Octavia thought they were doing. For she could see their little mouths opening and shutting, only she couldn't quite make out what they were trying to say to her. It all seemed a bit hazy. The Triplets weren't making it easy for her either, for they were all trying to speak at once, and of course when you do that it just gets you nowhere. So they decided, as Placido had the quietest voice, he would be their spokesperson. 'Go on,' urged the other two, 'tell her who we are and why we did what we did when Mrs Lines was playing a tune.' Placido felt nervous, which was unusual for him because he was meant to be the calmest of the three, quiet and unflappable. But he had never spoken to a human before, or one that seemed to be fast asleep, so he was feeling very unsure of himself. How did you address a human? 'Oh come on, get on with it,' said the other two, 'she'll be awake if you don't hurry.'

So Placido took a deep breath to steady his nerves and began. 'Excuse me,' he said very softly. 'Can you hear me?' But of course Octavia was in a deep sleep dreaming of little black and white men!

The little black and white men, as she looked at them more closely, looked like the black notes on her piano music. That is stupid, she thought dreamily, notes are notes, they don't want to speak to you! Placido though continued talking. 'We are called the Triplets. We don't want to harm you. We like your piano playing very much, but Mrs Lines, your piano teacher, well, we don't think she's a good teacher or a good player. We think she might be a fraud! That's why we did what we did, you see.'

Octavia really didn't see, and what did he say they did? It was beginning to become very confusing. Poco was by now fed up with how Placido was handling things, so he interrupted. 'It was us, we made the keys stick so they wouldn't play! We only did it to help you, we didn't mean to worry or upset you, or get Fortepiano into trouble!' Trouble, thought Octavia, how could you get a piano into trouble!

Then Poch decided he would have his say. 'It was my idea to make the keys stop working, you can blame it on me if you like!' Blame, it on you, Octavia thought, how can I blame anything on anyone when I don't know what they are talking about! But Poch carried on talking, he was by now becoming more and more worked up about it all. 'We don't want Fortepiano to be sent back to the workshop, it was us making his keys go wrong, he didn't do anything!'

Fortepiano, who had been listening to it all, sighed to himself. If only it had been me making the keys play, I'd be magic then, he thought! By now Octavia was beginning, in her dream, to get the picture, well sort of a picture! She had a piano who was disappointed it wasn't magic! And three little people living in it called Triplets, who did naughty things to the piano to stop it playing properly when they didn't like you! Come on, she said to herself, this is too strange to be real! 'So you see,' went on Poch, 'there is nothing wrong with Fortepiano, it is all our fault!'

Then they all said 'Sorry'. 'And we would like to stay on here,' they all remembered to add. Stay on, stay on where, thought Octavia, who was trying to get her brain in its very sleepy state round it all. Oh, for goodness sake, how can they stay inside my piano! They might stop it playing altogether, then where would I be!! I can't allow this . . . can't allow this . . . not my beautiful piano, and she kept mumbling this in her sleep!

Fortepiano could hear, just, what Octavia was mumbling. She still liked him, he thought; he wouldn't be sent away after all! 'I'll be a very good piano, Octavia, and I'll sound my best for you,' he said out loud. So loud in fact that it made him shake again on his big legs, and the Triplets nearly fell off his lid. Octavia's dream had just become stranger, now my piano is talking to me, she said to herself in her dream. But it's just a piano, it makes sounds, it can't talk! 'Well then,' she heard a little voice saying, it was Poco this time. 'Can we stay?'

'Mmmm,' she said sleepily, 's'pose so, stay for now . . . must behave though . . .' and she went into an even deeper sleep than before.

The Triplets nearly fell off the piano lid again, they were so pleased Octavia had said they could stay. They waved their little hats in the air jumping up at the same time with delight, then because they were on the lid, they all fell off backwards into the strings which made a huge 'donging' noise making Fortepiano's legs give a huge wobble! The Triplets were to stay! Fortepiano stood in his corner feeling very gloomy about this because he didn't believe for one minute they would behave themselves. Then he had a thought which brightened him up considerably. Octavia is asleep, when she wakens she won't remember what she said to the Triplets! And anyway if she does, she will think it was her dream. It was going to be all right!!

Chapter 29

Octavia woke up with a start to find her mother standing over her. 'Octavia, whatever are you doing down here?' Octavia felt a bit groggy, for she had been asleep on Fortepiano's lid for a few hours!

'I came down because I was worried about my piano not playing properly, and I must have fallen asleep.'

'Well,' replied her mother, 'off you go up to your room and get dressed, then we will have a talk about it all.'

So Octavia did as she was told, going slowly back upstairs to her room, when she got there she just flopped down on her bed, as she felt very tired and rather peculiar when she thought about it. She also didn't want to talk about her piano anymore to anyone, even her mother, because she knew it was working fine and she didn't want to have to explain why she knew. What she did want to do though was think about the dream she had just remembered she'd had. Only it didn't really feel like a dream, it felt very real. She remembered three very funny little men, Triplets they had said they were called. And they were, they said, living inside her piano! They had, they also said, been playing tricks on Mrs Lines when she was playing! That was why Octavia had thought there was something not quite right with Fortepiano. Oh no, she thought, this couldn't be real, there were no little people called Triplets, there were notes she had been playing called triplets! She definitely must have been having some very funny dream! She knew too that sometimes after a dream you felt it had really happened. Yes, she thought, that was it, problem solved, and she began to get dressed.

Now all the Triplets could think about was they were staying! Fortepiano, though, had other ideas. He was taking no more chances. He just had to find somewhere for the Triplets to go before they played any more of their tricks. So he sat in his corner thinking very hard about this problem, which, if only he had known, was going to work itself out very shortly!

Octavia, after she had dressed herself, went back downstairs to the kitchen for some breakfast. 'Now,' said her mother, 'you must be very worried about your piano if you got up in the middle of the night!' Octavia didn't want to talk about it, for her mind had been back thinking again about her dream which she couldn't quite shake off. She knew she would have to say something to her mother, or her father would be phoning Mr Sharp again and that would never do.

'I'm not worried anymore,' replied Octavia. 'I have played it, and there doesn't seem to be anything wrong, so you don't need to bother about it.'

'I'm pleased to hear it,' said Mrs Brown. 'But we still have the problem of what to do about your piano teacher. She says she won't come back to teach you if you don't get another piano!'

'Oh, but I'm not wanting it changed!' said Octavia in a panicky voice. 'I wouldn't part with my piano for anyone, and, it was a gift from Grandma.'

'Well, we will have to think of something,' her mother said. 'You need a teacher.' Mrs Brown was secretly relieved that Mrs Lines had made such a fuss, for she wasn't all that sure that when Mrs Lines had been playing, it was the piano's fault! So she set her mind to thinking about how she would look for another teacher, while Octavia, to get away from all her mother's questions, went back to the sitting-room to play her piano.

Chapter 30

Fortepiano was still puzzling over his problem when Octavia
came back into the sitting-room and started playing a tune.
It sounded rather sad and happy all at the same time; then in
the middle of the tune Octavia quite suddenly stopped
playing. 'It's such a relief that I won't have to send my lovely
piano back to Edinburgh,' she said out loud. And then just
as suddenly she started playing her tune again. Of course
Fortepiano was happy to hear what Octavia was thinking, but
it didn't solve his problem of what to do about the Triplets.

There was no problem for the Triplets though, for they
were quite beside themselves with happiness, they were
staying! To celebrate they were running all over the inside of
Fortepiano without a care in the world! They were so excited
and happy they had ignored the fact that Octavia was playing
a tune and Poco and Poch were again using the strings as a
swing park! The ones Octavia wasn't playing, of course.
Placido, well, he was doing what he liked best, calmly
sleeping in a corner! Poch was so happy he took a big risk,
he got bored of swinging and was now using the narrow edge

of Fortepiano to walk along, pretending it was a 'tightrope' just like in a circus! Poco shouted to him to be careful, he would fall off, but Poch just ignored him and went even further round the edge of the piano. 'Watch out, one wrong step and . . .' Poco didn't finish what he was about to say because, horror of horrors, that's just what happened! Poch felt himself falling faster and faster, down and down, then, when he thought he would crash onto the floor, there was a 'bump' and he found himself landing inside the old musical box Octavia had sitting on a lamp table beside the piano. Just as well the lid wasn't shut, he thought, as a big OUCH came from him. When he had dusted himself down and checked he was still in one piece and his hat was still on, he had a look around. It was quite cosy and roomy inside, with plenty of room for three! But wait a minute, what was he thinking, he must have bumped his head when he fell, for he was the only one there, the other two were, at this moment still up there, and he looked out of the box up to the top of Fortepiano. It looked very high from where he was standing, and he had just fallen all that way. It's a wonder I'm not just a blob of black and white dust now he thought, lucky Octavia had put the box there! Now he had a big problem, there was no way he could climb back up, and the other two wouldn't know where he was! He was very stuck!

Poco had heard the bump though, just after he had shouted to him to watch out, but where, thought Poco, had the bumpy noise come from? Surely Poch hadn't fallen all the way to the floor! So he very carefully climbed up onto the edge of Fortepiano and looked over. Poor Poch, he would be in some state if he had fallen all that way, he just couldn't bear to look, or could he? He looked right over, or as far as he dared without falling too. He couldn't believe what he was seeing, for there was Poch waving up to him from inside the musical box! He hadn't hurt himself after all, he was safe. Oh thank goodness, he thought to himself. But then he had another thought. Poch was down there, and Placido and himself were up there, he would have to think of something, but there was no way Poch would be able to climb back up. He would have to waken Placido, he would know what to do. So he very carefully climbed down off the edge of the piano and went to waken Placido, who wasn't very pleased at being woken up. 'Leave me alone, let me sleep,' he muttered to Poco, who was shaking him very hard.

'You can't sleep, you must waken up, something terrible has happened! Poch has fallen off the side of the piano!'

'What!' exclaimed Placido, and he jumped up so quickly he hit his head on the strings. 'Ouch,' he shouted, for his hat had fallen off when he jumped up. He found his hat and quickly put it back on. 'Where is he?' he asked Poco, sounding very concerned.

'Come on I'll show you, but you'll have to climb up onto the edge to see,' replied Poco, and he dragged Placido over and up onto the edge so he could look over. Placido very carefully looked over, for he didn't like heights. Then as he looked down he saw Poch waving to him from the musical box.

'How on earth did he manage to get there?'

'Oh he was being his usual silly self and pretending he was walking a tightrope,' answered Poco.

'What a very stupid thing to do,' said Placido as he looked back down again trying not to feel dizzy.

Poch waved up to him and shouted 'It's quite nice down here, want to come and join me?!' Of all the stupid things to do, and now he wants us to join him, thought Placido. Then he climbed off the edge for a moment to let him think properly about the problem. If Poch couldn't get back up then their only option was to go down to him, but how! There seemed to be only the one solution and that was to jump! So he told Poco what he thought they could do. Poco was just as horrified as he was at the thought of jumping, for if they missed the musical box they would most certainly crash onto the floor, then there would be two black and white blobs on the carpet for Mrs Brown or Octavia to find!

'We just can't,' said Poco by now feeling nothing less than terrified.

'We'll have to if we want to see Poch again,' said Placido, feeling very frightened too. They both thought about it for a moment longer. 'If Poch did it, then we'll just have to, and be careful that we land in the box and not the floor!' Placido said.

'Then let's do it,' said Poco, not wanting to take too long to think about it, and before Placido could reply Poco was standing on the edge and before he could shout out a warning, he had jumped! Poco felt himself whizzing through the air very fast, and then he felt a bump. He had shut his eyes for he didn't want to see where he was going. When he opened them it was to find Poch looking at him with a very worried look on his face.

'Are you all right, you flew down very fast, I thought you would go right past me.'

'What do you mean?' said Poco.

'Well I was waiting to catch you but you just seemed to fall in the right direction,' said Poch.

'Thank goodness for that,' said Poco, by now feeling a bit better, but feeling very sore and a bit dazed. Then he remembered that Placido was still up on the edge, Poco had quite surprised him by taking off so quickly.

They both looked up to where Placido was balanced very precariously on the edge of Fortepiano. 'Come on,' they both shouted to him. 'It'll be fine, we will catch you!' But Placido wasn't so sure about it all now, he could think of lots of reasons why he should just stay where he was, he would get lots of peace and quiet to sleep for a start, but on the other hand if he didn't go then he would be all alone, and it might get too lonely without the others. 'Oh come on, hurry up,' Poco and Poch both shouted. 'We will count up to three, then just jump!' Placido still hesitated. 'One, two, three!' and before Placido could think about it anymore he did just that. He went flying into space, he could feel all the air rushing past as he flew down and down, then there was another bump, and this time a loud howl, as Placido landed right on top of the other two! When they had all got their breaths back, dusted themselves down and checked to see there was nothing broken, they all set off to have a look through their new home. It was all going to be very exciting, or so they thought!

Chapter 31

Fortepiano sighed, what a relief, they had done it! Fortepiano couldn't bear to watch as Poco and Placido had jumped off his side! He had felt rather upset when he saw Poch fall off, for he was quite sure he would go all the way to the ground and hurt himself, thank goodness for the musical box sitting on the table, he was in no doubt whatsoever that it had saved Poch from a very bad fall indeed. At least now he was rid of those naughty Triplets, well he hoped he was; they had gone and he hadn't had to do anything! Maybe he would get some peace and quiet, and Octavia would be left alone. He hoped so.

Octavia of course had been practising her tunes, quite oblivious to the 'goings on' inside her piano! Her dream now didn't seem quite so real as before, as dreams tend to fade away as the day or days go by. It was all a bit far fetched really when you thought about it, having little people talk to you! She was going to concentrate very hard on her practising for she didn't know yet who was going to give her piano lessons, it certainly wouldn't be Mrs Lines, she was sure of that!

'Octavia,' said her mother coming into the sitting-room, she was sounding quite excited about something, thought Octavia. 'You will never guess, I have found you another piano teacher, but you'll never guess who it is!' she said. Octavia had just been thinking about this problem when her mother had come in to the room, she really needed to find a new teacher, but she was dreading it. The next teacher might be more horrible than Mrs Lines! 'Come on Octavia, stop dreaming,' said Mrs Brown. 'Guess who your new teacher will be?' Octavia just wanted to be left alone to practise.

She didn't want to have to think about what horrible teacher she might have to put up with next, and she was by now becoming fed up with her mother's guessing games! 'Oh I don't know,' she replied quite crossly. Mrs Brown seemed to take a deep breath and then she said, ' It's your Grandma!' There was a moment's silence in the room while Octavia tried to take this momentous announcement in.

'She can't, Grandma lives in Edinburgh. I hope that doesn't mean that we are moving,' she said quite crossly.

'Oh of course not, don't be so silly Octavia,' said her mother, who was becoming a bit impatient with Octavia by now. 'We didn't want to say anything till it was all settled, but Grandpa and Grandma are coming to stay here for good. They have bought a new house right here in the village. And when I told your Grandma what had been happening at your lessons, she offered to teach you herself!'

This was very big news for Octavia to take in. She knew now that Grandma had once been a famous piano player, and for a while a teacher, and now Grandma would be teaching her! Octavia was so pleased and excited all at once, she jumped up off the piano stool and ran over and gave her mother a big joyous hug! It felt like it was her birthday all over again! 'I'm glad you are so pleased,' said her mother. 'Now you had better get lots of practising in before Grandma moves here. She will be looking for a big improvement from the last time!' and Mrs Brown went to make a celebratory cup of tea for she was very pleased not only for Octavia but also for the fact that they would all be together again. No more Mrs Lines, thought Octavia, for she was sure there was something strange about her. So Octavia went back to playing her beloved Fortepiano, happy in the knowledge another problem had been solved!

'A Little Note'

Mrs Lines was sitting in her little cottage feeling rather irritated. She had lost one of her best pupils (not that she would have told anyone that). She wouldn't be asked back again to teach Octavia. Mr Brown had made that quite clear when he had telephoned her earlier. He hadn't been at all impressed by the way she had handled things at Octavia's last lesson and he had given her the feeling that she wasn't good at her job. When she had thought about it afterwards she had realised there was something quite strange about everything that had happened at some of the lessons. And of course for their part the Triplets had thought Mrs Lines wasn't all that she seemed! And they were quite right about that.

For Mrs Lines wasn't all that she seemed! Mrs Lines had a 'big secret' which she very much hoped would stay that way, but it was very difficult for her sometimes to keep control of her 'big secret'. She had lived in the village for some time, but she always knew that her past might catch up with her sooner or later. Each time she had thought she had found a good place to live, she had eventually been forced to move somewhere else, and eventually she had ended up living in the same village as Octavia.

Would her 'big secret' mean she might have to move again, only time would tell. She would have to be more careful now, and make sure she took enough of her 'spell' so her pupils wouldn't begin to guess who she really was! She would have to be on the alert all the time now, for she really liked her little cottage and didn't want to have to move again in order to keep her 'big secret'.

But secrets sometimes have a way of revealing themselves and might be stumbled upon by some person quite accidentally . . .